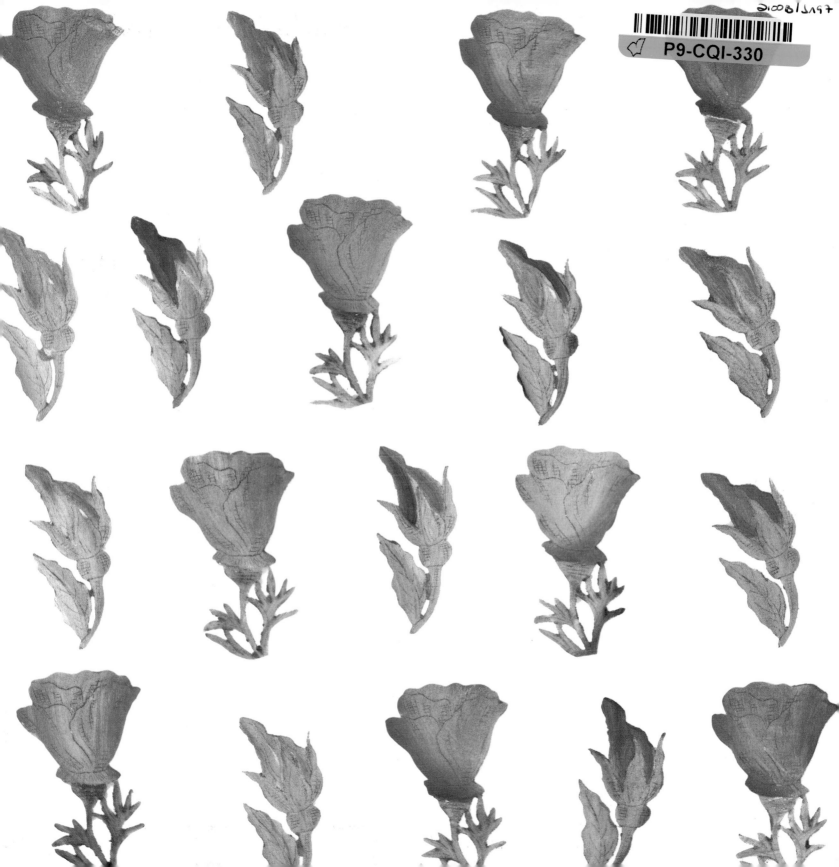

Wildflower ABC

HARCOURT BRACE & COMPANY

San Diego   New York   London

DIANA POMEROY

Wildflower ABC

AN ALPHABET OF POTATO PRINTS

With special thanks to Linda Lockowitz, Michelle Lodjic,
Denise Nakagawa, and Betty and Gary at Documounts Framing

Requests for permission to make copies of any part of the work
should be mailed to: Permissions Department, Harcourt Brace & Company,
6277 Sea Harbor Drive, Orlando, Florida 32887-6777.

Library of Congress Cataloging-in-Publication Data
Pomeroy, Diana.
Wildflower ABC: an alphabet of potato prints/Diana Pomeroy.
p. cm.
Includes glossary and bibliographical references.
Summary: Presents potato-print illustrations for wildflowers for every letter
of the alphabet, with all sorts of information about each flower.
ISBN 0-15-201041-6
1. Wildflowers—United States—Juvenile literature.
2. Wildflowers—Juvenile literature. 3. Wildflowers—Folklore.
4. English language—Alphabet—Juvenile literature.
5. Potato printing—Juvenile literature. [1. Wildflowers. 2. Alphabet.]
I. Title.
QK115.P65 1997
582.13[E]—dc20   96-19748
Printed in Mexico
First edition
A C E F D B

 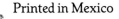
The illustrations in this book were done with 40-count potatoes
and acrylic paints printed and appliquéd on 200-count cotton muslin.
The display and text type were set in Worcester.
Color separations by Pica Colour Separation Pte. Ltd., Singapore
Printed and bound by RR Donnelley & Sons Company, Reynosa, Mexico
This book was printed on Patina Matte paper.
Production supervision by Stanley Redfern and Ginger Boyer
Designed by Linda Lockowitz

34, 587

To my 40-count mom
and my sister Teddie

Aa
Aster

Bluebonnet
Bb

Columbine

Cc

Dandelion
Dd

Elecampane
Ee

Firecracker

Ff

G g Gourd

Honeysuckle
Hh

I i Iris

Jimsonweed
Jj

K k
Knapweed

Lily

Ll

Mm
Morning glory

Nasturtium

Nn

Orchid
Oo

P p
Poppy

Queen
Anne's lace
Q q

Rudbeckia
Rr

Strawberry
Ss

Trillium

T t

Uu
Urtica
diocia

Vetch
V v

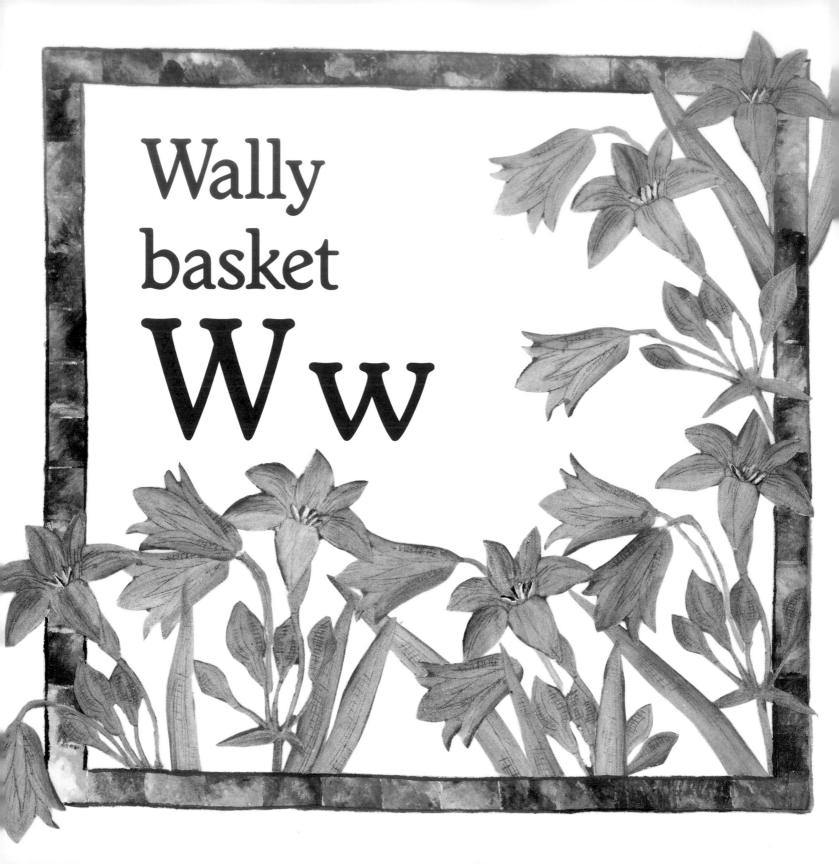

Wally
basket
Ww

X x
Xerophyllum tenax

Yarrow Y y

Zigadenus
fremontii
Z z

More about Wildflowers

Aster: *(Aster)* Compositae (sunflower) family. In Greek legend the aster was created from stardust by the tears of Virgo as they fell to earth. In medieval France and Germany asters were burned to keep away evil spirits.

Bluebonnet: *(Lupinus subcarnosus)* Leguminosae (pea) family. Common name: wild lupine. *Lupinus* comes from the Latin *lupus,* meaning "wolf." It was believed that lupines robbed nutrients from the soil, just as wolves robbed the shepherd of his sheep. In fact, lupines enrich the soil by adding nitrogen. The species *Lupinus texenis* is the state flower of Texas.

Columbine: *(Aquilegia canadensis)* Ranunculaceae (buttercup) family. The word *columbine* comes from *columbinus,* in Latin "dove." The Victorians believed columbine was a symbol of folly and the deserted lover. It was an insult to give it to a woman and bad luck to give it to a man. Rocky Mountain columbine is the state flower of Colorado.

Dandelion: *(Taraxacum officinale)* Compositae family. Common names: blowball, cankerwort, swine snout. Dandelion seeds can travel more than five miles from the plant. Folklore has it that blowing off all a dandelion's seeds in one breath will make a wish come true. The number of seeds left after blowing tells the time of day and how many children you will have.

Elecampane: *(Inula helenium)* Compositae family. Common names: elfdock, elfwort, scabwort, wild sunflower. Elecampane is said to have sprung from the tears of Helen of Troy.

Firecracker: *(Dichelostemma ida-maia)* Lilaceae family. These flowers resemble loose clusters of firecrackers tied by their fuses.

Gourd: Cucurbitaceae (cucumber) family. Common names: wild cucumber, stinking gourd. Anglo-Saxon herbals from the sixteenth century prescribe laying a long gourd or cucumber in the cradle of a sleeping infant "sick of an ague" so "it shall very quickly be made whole."

Honeysuckle: *(Diervilla lonicera)* Caprifoliaceae family. To the Victorians, honeysuckle meant devoted affection. It was once used widely in medicine but is now prized primarily for perfume. Children love to suck the sweet nectar from the base of the florets.

Iris: *(Iridaceae cristata)* Iridaceae family. The iris was named by the Greeks for the goddess of the rainbow. Iris was a messenger of the gods, portrayed as a lovely young woman in a multicolored robe, carrying a herald staff. It was her duty to lead the souls of dead women across the rainbow bridge to the Elysian Fields. Iris is the state flower of Tennessee.

Jimsonweed: *(Datura stramonium)* Solanaceae (nightshade) family. The common name is a corruption of "Jamestown weed," named because many soldiers, sent there to stop Bacon's Rebellion in 1676, were poisoned when they ran out of food and ate the fruit of the poisonous hallucinogenic plant.

Knapweed: *(Centaurea maculosa)* Compositae family. Knapweed is derived from the German word *knopf,* which means bump or button. English girls wore them as a sign of eligibility. It was also believed that if a girl hid this flower in her apron, she could have the bachelor of her choice.

Lily: Lilaceae family. Jupiter gave a sleeping potion to Juno, queen of the gods, and placed the infant Hercules at her breast so the divine milk would render Hercules immortal. As the baby drank, drops fell from the sky, passing through the heavens to create the Milky Way and falling to earth, creating white lilies.

Morning glory: *(Convolvulus sepium)* Convolvulaceae family. Common name: bindweed. According to a Japanese story, a poet, Kaga-no-Chiyojo, found her well bucket overgrown with morning glory vines. Instead of disturbing the plant, she begged her neighbor for water; hence the morning glory signifies the love of nature.

Nasturtium: *(Tropaeolum majus)* Tropaeolaceae family. Nasturtiums were introduced to Europe from Peru by the conquistadors. Sailors took barrels of the pickled seeds on long voyages and ate them like capers to prevent scurvy. Nasturtiums stood for patriotism in Victorian times.

Orchid: Orchidaceae family. These elaborate flowers have a highly specialized relationship with pollinators. Their pollen is held together in masses, making it difficult for an insect to position itself to pick up pollen and carry it to another flower, which is why orchids are rare. One member of the orchid family is the calypso, named for the sea nymph who detained Odysseus on his return from Troy in Homer's *Odyssey*.

Poppy: Papaveraceae family. The Egyptians used poppies in funerals and burial rituals. The Romans used the juice for witchcraft, particularly to ease the pain of love. The Greeks used the flowers to honor the shrines of Demeter, goddess of fertility. The seeds were also used as a love charm and put in wine to bring strength and health to Olympic athletes.

Queen Anne's lace: *(Daucus carota)* Umbelliferae family. Common name: wild carrot. The flowering heads served eighteenth-century English courtiers as "living lace." It is a member of the parsley family. Old legend says parsley takes so long to germinate because it goes to the devil nine times before growing through the ground; to slight the devil, parsley should be planted on Good Friday.

Rudbeckia: Compositae (sunflower) family. Common name: coneflower. The flower is named in honor of the famed Swedish botanist Olof Rudbeck and his son Olof.

Strawberry: *(Fragaria vesca)* Rosaceae (rose) family. The word *strawberry* comes from the Anglo-Saxon *streawberige*, referring to the berries "strewing" their runners over the ground. They are associated with the planet Venus and the astrological sign Libra.

Trillium: *(Trillium grandiflorum)* Liliaceae family. Women used trillium as a love potion by boiling the root and putting it in the food of the man they desired. A Native American story tells of a young girl who wanted the chief's son for her husband but tripped and dropped her potion into the food of an ugly old man, who chased her for months, continually asking her to marry him. Endangered throughout the United States, trillium takes seven years to grow to flowering size and should, therefore, never be picked.

Urtica diocia: Urticaceae family. Common name: stinging nettle. In Algonquian myth, Sirakitehak, who created heaven and earth, invented nettle nets after watching a spider spin its web. She told the women to twist the fibers on their thighs to make netting, which they still do to this day.

Vetch: *(Vicia americana)* Leguminosae (pea) family. Vetch can be used by a newcomer to determine the past weather common to a particular area: If vetch blooms in March, the winter was mild; if the winter was harsh, vetch will not bloom until later.

Wally basket: *(Brodiaea elegans)* Liliaceae (lily) family. Grassnut, or Ithuriel's spear *(Brodiaea laxa),* grows on heavy soils in grasslands or brush from southern Oregon to southern California.

Xerophyllum tenax: Liliaceae (lily) family. Common names: bear grass, Indian basket grass, elk grass, turkey beard, bear lily, pine lily. Native Americans ate the roasted rootstock and used the leaves to weave clothing and baskets.

Yarrow: *(Achillea millefolium)* The Latin name honors Achilles, who carried the plant with him and used its wound-healing powers on his men during the Trojan War. Yarrow stops bleeding and heals bruises and burns. For Victorians, yarrow meant war.

Zigadenus fremontii: Liliaceae family. Common name: camas. Camas are infamous for poisoning livestock and people, who mistake the bulbs of such poisonous species as death camas *(Zigadenus venenosus)* for those of edible ones like the camas lily *(Camassia).*

Bibliography

Lust, John. *The Herb Book.* New York: Bantam Books, 1974.

Mabey, Richard. *The New Age Herbalist.* New York: Collier Books, Macmillan Publishing, 1988.

Martin, Laura C. *Garden Flower Folklore.* Old Saybrook, Connecticut: The Globe Pequot Press, 1987.

Martin, Laura C. *Wildflower Folklore.* Old Saybrook, Connecticut: The Globe Pequot Press, 1986.

Mercatante, Anthony S. *The Magic Garden: The Myths and Folklore of Flowers, Plants, Trees, and Herbs.* New York: Harper & Row, 1976.

Rohde, Eleanour Sinclair. *The Old English Herbals.* New York: Dover Publications, Inc., 1971.

Weed, Susan. *The Wise Woman Herbal: Healing Wise.* Woodstock, New York: Ash Tree Publishing, 1989.